DORLING KINDERSLEY CLASSICS

THE
ODYSSEY

Dorling **DK** Kindersley

A RETELLING FOR YOUNG READERS

Produced by Leapfrog Press Ltd

Project Editor Alastair Dougall
Art Editor Ness Wood

For Dorling Kindersley
Senior Editor Alastair Dougall
Managing Art Editor Jacquie Gulliver
Picture Research Liz Moore
Production Chris Avgherinos
DTP Designer Sue Wright

Published in the United States by Dorling Kindersley Publishing, Inc.
95 Madison Avenue, New York, New York 10016

First American Edition, 2000
2 468109 753

Copyright © 2000 Dorling Kindersley Limited

Text copyright © 2000 Adrian Mitchell
Illustrations copyright © 2000 Stuart Robertson
Compilation copyright © 2000 Dorling Kindersley Limited

Library of Congress Cataloging-in-Publication Data

Mitchell, Adrian.
  The Odyssey / by Homer ; adapted by Adrian Mitchell.--1st American ed.
    p. cm. – (Dorling Kindersley classics)
Summary: A retelling of Homer's epic that describes the wanderings of Odysseus after
the fall of Troy. Illustrated notes throughout the text explain the historical background
of the story.
  ISBN 0-7894-5455-7
  1. Odysseus (Greek mythology)—Juvenile literature. [1. Odysseus (Greek mythology)
2. Mythology, Greek] I. Homer. Odyssey. II. Title. III. Series.
BL820.O3 M58 2000
883'.01
                                                          99-043280

Color reproduction by Dot Gradations Limited
Printed and bound in Hong Kong by Dai Nippon Printing Co. Ltd.

See our complete catalog at
www.dk.com

DORLING KINDERSLEY CLASSICS

THE ODYSSEY

ADRIAN MITCHELL

Illustrated by
STUART ROBERTSON

DK

A Dorling Kindersley Book

LONDON, NEW YORK, SYDNEY, DELHI, PARIS
MUNICH and JOHANNESBURG

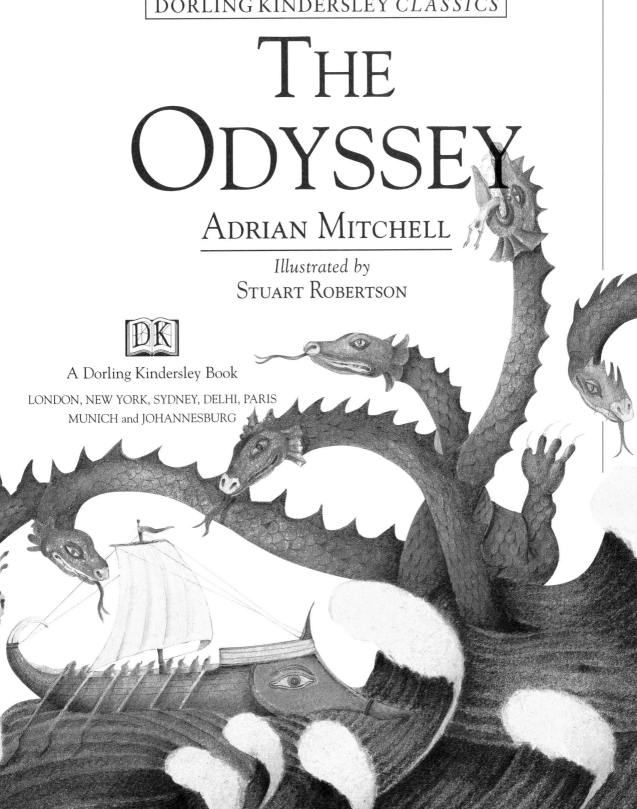

CONTENTS

———◆◆———

Penelope

Odysseus

INTRODUCTION 6

THE TROJAN WAR 8

Chapter one
TO BE A HERO 10

Chapter two
THE LOTUS EATERS 12

Chapter three
THE CYCLOPS 14

Chapter four
THE ISLE OF WINDS 22

Chapter five
CANNIBAL ISLAND 24

Chapter six
CIRCE 26

Chapter seven
THE ENCHANTED ENCHANTRESS 28

Telemachus   Circe   Calypso   Polyphemus   Zeus

GODS AND GODDESSES 30

Chapter eight
THE LAND OF THE DEAD 32

Chapter nine
THE SIRENS 36

Chapter ten
SCYLLA AND CHARYBDIS 38

Chapter eleven
CALYPSO'S ISLAND 42

Chapter twelve
NAUSICAA 46

Chapter thirteen
THE HOMECOMING 48

Chapter fourteen
ODYSSEUS'S REVENGE 52

Chapter fifteen
HUSBAND AND WIFE 58

ODYSSEUS'S VOYAGE 62

Hermes

Tiresias

Nausicaa

Athene

The Sirens

INTRODUCTION

Composed by the Greek poet Homer, probably during the second half of the 8th century BC, and preserved by word of mouth for centuries before being written down, *The Odyssey* is one of the greatest works in world literature. Its influence on writers, poets, and painters has been immense, and shows no signs of abating. The events of the story are so vivid that sites all over the Mediterranean region have become linked with the legend, and attempts have been made by modern voyagers to follow in the wake of Odysseus and his crew.

The Odyssey's timeless appeal is remarkable, but not so hard to understand: though nearly two thousand years old, it is a fast-paced, seafaring adventure, a tale of exotic lands, terrible storms, blissful calms, and horrifying monsters. It has an enthralling, supernatural atmosphere: the gods leave their realms in humble disguise to involve themselves in human affairs, magic spells are cast, terrible curses are sworn, and strange predictions come true. But, perhaps most telling of all, the story has a sympathetic, complex, and very human hero in Odysseus himself, a man who, as we shall see, never, ever wanted to leave his beloved wife, son, and homeland in the first place!

Tim Severin and the crew of *Argo* follow Odysseus's course in 1986.

The Trojan War

The legendary war between the Greeks and the city of Troy was caused by the abduction of Helen, wife of the Greek King Menelaus, by Paris, a Trojan prince. It lasted ten years and claimed the lives of many great warriors, whose deeds were celebrated by the poet Homer in *The Iliad*. Until the late 1900s, people assumed that Troy had never existed; but then the German archaeologist Heinrich Schliemann made an amazing discovery.

Poet of war
Homer's *The Iliad*, movingly described the tragedy of war as well as the heroism of the combatants.

This gold death mask, found at Mycenae, was once believed to show the face of Agamemnon.

Leader of the Greeks
The Greeks were led by Agamemnon, king of Mycena who was Menelaus's brother. army comprised the finest warriors, including wise Odyss

The Judgment of Paris
The seeds of war were sown when Paris gave first prize to Aphrodite, goddess of love, in a beauty contest between her, Athene, goddess of wisdom, and Hera, queen of the gods. As a reward, Aphrodite offered him any woman he wanted. He stole off to Troy with Helen, wife of King Menelaus of Sparta.

Black ship
Bent on revenge, the Greek kings gathered their men and ships and set sail for Troy.

Bitter struggle
The war dragged on for year afte year. Many brave deeds were don many champions died; but both si were too proud to end the fightin

Achilles and Hector

One of the war's most decisive battles was between Achilles, the Greeks' champion, and Hector, champion of the Trojans. Achilles won, and triumphantly dragged Hector's body around the walls of Troy.

Athene, goddess of wisdom, a supporter of the Greeks, puts finishing touches to the Trojan Horse

The Trojan Horse

With no end to the war in sight, the Greeks turned to their most cunning leader, Odysseus. He suggested that the army build a giant wooden horse and hide a group of armed men within it. The rest of the men should sail out of sight of the walls of Troy and wait.

The fall of Troy

The Trojans assumed that the large wooden horse the Greeks had left behind was an offering to a god. They dragged it inside the city walls. At nightfall the men hidden inside the horse crept out and opened the gates to the rest of the Greek army. Troy was utterly destroyed.

Helen of Troy

When King Menelaus found his wife Helen, he was on the verge of killing her, until Odysseus pleaded for her life. With her lover Paris long since dead, Menelaus forgave her, and took her back to Sparta.

THE DISCOVERY OF TROY

For much of his life archaeologist Heinrich Schliemann (1822–90) had loved The Iliad. Determined to prove Troy was no myth, he started digging at Hissarlik in Turkey in 1870. His excavations ultimately revealed a city – or rather several cities – called Troy. It had really existed.

Unlucky mistake

Schliemann incorrectly assumed that the oldest remains were of Troy. Yet his discovery encouraged others to explore the site.

Site of Troy

The site revealed the remains of nine towns. The seventh oldest, dating from the 13th century BC, was the Troy of legend.

The oracle at Delphi
*When a Greek needed advice
on the future he would
consult an oracle – a wise
person with powers of
prophecy. The oracle at
Delphi was the most famous
of all. Sometimes the oracle's
words had double meanings,
but in Odysseus's case the
advice is very clear.*

Chapter one

TO BE A HERO

ODYSSEUS DIDN'T WANT to be a hero. War was coming, dark and powerful as a thunderstorm. But Odysseus wanted to stay home. He loved his wife Penelope, his baby son Telemachus, and his old mother and father. He loved his fine house and farm on the rocky Greek island of Ithaca.

Why should he sail far over the raging seas to attack the high-walled city of Troy? The great oracle had foretold that if he did, he would not return home for twnty years. And why risk his life to rescue Helen, the beautiful bride of the Greek King Menelaus, who had run off with some Trojan prince?

But Menelaus needed the brave and strong Odysseus in his army. So up from the beach to the rocky farm climbed King Menelaus with his friend Palamedes, determined to recruit Odysseus, the most cunning of all the Greeks.

Odysseus had seen their ship arriving. He decided to outwit them by pretending to be out of his wits – far too crazy to go to war.

He harnessed a small donkey and a huge ox together to pull his plow. He shoved his puppy Argus in the front pocket of his leather apron, stuck a ridiculous cap on his head and began to plow, walkin backward.

King Menelaus was startled to see Odysseus stumbling over the field, spitting gravel and sowing handfuls of salt instead of grain.

"Poor man," said the king, "He's far gone."

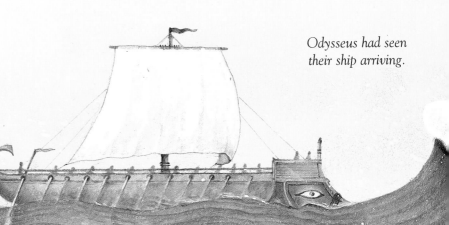

*Odysseus had seen
their ship arriving.*

Palamedes was not so sure. He knew Odysseus and his tricks and decided to test him. He snatched the baby Telemachus from the arms of his nurse Eurycleia and placed him on the ground in front of the advancing plow.

Penelope screamed. Odysseus turned and saw his son about to be crushed. He pulled at the leather reins with all his strength, dragging the donkey and ox to a halt.

Menelaus laughed. "If you're sane enough to save your son, you're sane enough to fight the Trojans." Even Odysseus had to laugh. But then he had to say goodbye to his family, and his home.

Off to war he sailed, thinking he would return before the next harvest. But it was a long war. However hard they fought, the Greek army could not break into the fortified city of Troy.

The siege of the city lasted for ten bloodstained years. Then the clever Odysseus invented a giant wooden horse. It was left as a gift for the Trojans, who wheeled it into their city. But the horse contained Odysseus and the greatest of the Greek warriors. That night they climbed down from the horse's belly, set fire to the city of Troy – and the long war was over.

Longing to be home as soon as possible, Odysseus set sail with a fleet of twelve fine ships.

Childhood scar

Odysseus had a carefree childhood roaming the hills with his dog Argus. But one day, to the distress of his family and nurse Eurycleia, he was wounded in the thigh during a boar hunt. The wound healed, but left a tell-tale scar.

Fruit of forgetfulness
The lotus is sacred in Egypt, India, and China. Eating the fruit of the lotus in this story makes a person completely forget home, friends, and family.

Fearless sailor
The Greeks loved stories about adventurous voyagers. Another famous myth tells of Jason (here played by Todd Armstrong in a 1963 film), who sailed in search of the Golden Fleece.

Chapter two

THE LOTUS EATERS

A STRONG SEA-WIND drove Odysseus and his fleet to the town of Ismarus on the coast of Thrace. The Thracians had fought against the Greeks in the Trojan War. Landing by moonlight, the sailors took their revenge on the town by killing and looting all night long.

But Odysseus made them spare Maron, for he was the priest of Apollo, and it is wise to avoid offending the gods. Gratefully, Maron presented Odysseus with gold, silver, and twelve jars of the finest blood-red wine.

Odysseus sensed it was time to leave the town. But most of his crew lay drunk and snoring in the streets. Meanwhile the Thracians roused their cousins, the Hairy Men from the Hills, a wild and warlike tribe. Hurling a hailstorm of bronze-tipped spears, the Hairy Men chased Odysseus and his men back to their ships and out to sea. Odysseus lost seventy-two of his men that night.

His ships headed for home, but a terrible gale arose, hurling them off course and tearing their sails to rags. When the storm dropped, the men cheered as they saw a green and yellow desert island sleeping under a summer-blue sky.

Three snowy mountains rose above deep forests. From the high cliffs, streams fell in waterfalls like downward smoke. Odysseus sent three of his men to investigate this promising land.

They saw a desert island sleeping under a summer-blue sky.

They met a group of smiling,
brown-eyed men and women.

Crossing the beach, they met a group of smiling, brown-eyed men and women who welcomed them, inviting them to sit with them on the sand and eat the fruit of the lotus.

The sailors didn't know it, but whoever tastes that honey-tasting fruit loses all desire to go home. All he wants is to watch the sun sink into the sea and the moon climb up to its place among the stars while he reclines and feasts upon the lotus for the rest of his life. For the lotus fills the brain with colorful pictures and sweet music. Soon the real world is as forgotten as last night's dream.

Those men would have been lost forever. But Odysseus followed them ashore. His three old comrades stared at him like a stranger. A tall woman offered a plate of glowing fruit.

But Odysseus pushed her aside. "Back to your ships!" he shouted, but his men smiled, giggled, and nodded their heads to the music of the Lotus Eaters.

Odysseus took off his leather belt. He strapped it around the three dreamers and dragged them back to the shore. Despite their howls of protest, he hauled them onboard his ship and ordered the fleet to sail. And he did not free those men till they were out of sight and sound of the beguiling Island of the Lotus Eaters.

Chapter three

THE CYCLOPS

THE WIND DROPPED and died. The men rowed smoothly over the blue mirror of the sea. Soon they arrived at a wooded island swarming with wild goats.

The sailors jumped ashore, long spears in their hands. Soon the skinned and oiled bodies of a hundred goats were roasting.

All that day Odysseus and his men feasted. But the good goat-smoke drifted uphill, in through the opening of a large cave and up into the nostrils of a monstrous creature. And the monster sniffed, snorted, and shuffled to the mouth of his cave.

The next morning Odysseus pointed up the hill. "Good friends," he said. "Stay onboard while I take twelve men to explore this land and find out if its people are fierce or friendly."

So he and his men scrambled up the hill, which is the home of the Cyclopes, carrying food and a wineskin full of strong, blood-red wine, a gift of the priest Maron.

They pushed through a flock of tame sheep and goats and found themselves standing in the dark mouth of a cave. Lighting a flaming torch, they entered cautiously and gazed around.

The cavern was like a dark and grisly dairy. There were cheeses as big as cartwheels and enormous buckets of buttermilk. In the corner was a heap of dry bones – sheep bones, goat bones, and human bones.

Goat herds
Greece's rough grazing is well suited to goats, which provide cheese, called feta, milk, meat, and skins for clothing. This bronze goat dates from 500 BC.

The Cyclopes
A race of one-eyed giants, the Cyclopes forged the thunderbolts that were Zeus's most powerful weapons. The Cyclopes were hugely strong and bad-tempered. They had little respect for gods, and none for human beings.

Most of the sailors wanted to drive the sheep and goats down to their ship and sail away.

"No," said Odysseus, "Let's stay and meet the owner of this amazing cave."

So they sat down and helped themselves to some cheese. But then came a noise like a walking earthquake. A giant strode into the cave driving his sheep and goats before him, prodding them with a tree-sized walking stick.

As the huge creature turned in the light from the entrance, Odysseus and his men saw that he was a Cyclops – a giant with only one eye – an eye that glared from the middle of his forehead. The giant closed the entrance of the cave with an enormous wheel of solid rock. Then he sat down and milked his ewes and nannygoats, singing horribly to himself. He placed the brimming pails in a cool puddle. Then he sat down with a sigh and lit a fire. And by the light of the flames he saw Odysseus and his men.

A giant strode into the cave driving his sheep and goats before him.

*He grabbed two men and
swung them through the air.*

"Strangers!" the Cyclops boomed. "Who be you?"

"We are Greeks," said Odysseus. "We were sailing home from Troy, but we lost our way. You know what the great Zeus commands – strangers should always be greeted kindly and fed generously."

"Strangerman," said the Cyclops. "You be fool. We Cyclopes spit on Zeus. We spit on all gods. Cyclopes stronger than gods. I show you how strong. I show you – cheese-thievers!"

The Cyclops jumped to his feet. He grabbed two men by their feet, swung them through the air and smashed their skulls like eggs on the limestone floor of the cave. Then he tore them to pieces with his hands before devouring them – flesh, blood, bones, and all. He washed down this mess with a pail of buttermilk, then lay down beside the fire and began to snore like ten lions.

Polyphemus's cave?
Some legends make Sicily the home of the Cyclopes. A cave at Trapani could have been Polyphemus's lair.

Greek hospitality
The Greeks believed in showing hospitality to strangers. It was a serious crime to show disrespect to – never mind murder and devour! – harmless visitors.

Odysseus felt for his sword. Perhaps he could creep up on the sleeping giant and stab him through the heart. But then he and his crew would starve to death in the cave, trapped forever by the great wheel of rock sealing the door. For only a giant or a god could shift that heavy rock. All that night Odysseus lay awake, plotting revenge and escape. The next morning the Cyclops lit his fire and milked his beasts and growled his awful milking song. Then, with a smile like an open grave, he snatched up two more men, toasted them over his fire, crunched them up, and swallowed them down.

Next he drove his sheep and goats from the cave, blocking the entrance behind him with the great wheel of rock. The sailors heard his footsteps stomping off down the path to the meadows below.

Odysseus gazed around the gloomy cave, refusing to despair.

Suddenly he noticed that the Cyclops had left his huge walking stick in the cave. It was made of green olive-wood and was tall as the mast of a great ship. From this, Odysseus cut a length about the height of a man. He ordered his crew to carve it into the shape of a spear. With the blade of his sword, he shaved the shaft into a wicked point and hardened that point in the fire. Then he hid the spear under the dung that covered most of the cave's floor like a stinking carpet.

Odysseus smiled at his terrified men. "We'll wait till he's asleep tonight," he whispered. "And then we'll strike."

The Cyclops snatched up two more men and toasted them over his fire.

As the red sun set, the Cyclops returned. He drove in his flocks, closed his stone wheel of a door, and milked the sheep and goats. Then he grinned like a skull, slaughtered two more men, and ate them.

Odysseus filled a wooden wine bowl with the blood-red wine of Maron, and offered it to him "Here, Cyclops, try washing down your meal with some of our good wine. I brought it as a gift, hoping you'd help us find our way home."

"No go home. But good wine," said the Cyclops, gulping it down.

"Have some more," said Odysseus, refilling the bowl.

"Good," said the Cyclops, swilling it down, licking his bulging lips and feeling suddenly friendly. "My name be Polyphemus. Give more wine. Tell your name. I give you good gift."

So Odysseus refilled the bowl and said: "My name is Nobody."

"Nobody," said the Cyclops. "Good. Polyphemus eat all the others first, Nobody last. That your good gift." And the Cyclops laughed with a sound like a great pine tree falling. Then, full of human flesh and strong wine, he fell asleep.

As the Cyclops lay on his back with his huge eye shut, Odysseus drew the sharpened pole from under the dung. He heated it in the fire until it glowed red. Then he and his companions grasped the pole and thrust it deep into the eye of the Cyclops. The pole hissed like a red-hot poker stuck in a bucket of water. Polyphemus screamed and twisted the stak out of his eye. He stumbled to the door of his cave.

"Help!" yelled the blinded Cyclops. "Help me, brother Cyclopes!"

He blundered around yelling and screeching until the other Cyclopes who lived nearby came lumbering up to his cave.

"What is wrong, Polyphemus?" boomed their leader, Arompes. "We al sleeping happy. You wake us shouting. Is robbers robbing your sheep? Do murdermen attack you? What wrong?"

Polyphemus cried out to them: "Nobody is killing me!"

"Who fight you, then?"

"Nobody is attacking me!" screamed Polyphemus in his agony. "Nobody is hurting me!"

"Oh, that's all right then," said Arompes. "Come on, Cyclops, ome to bed."

"No – stay!" cried Polyphemus. "Stay and catch Nobody!"

"I think you sick, Polyphemus," said Arompes. "Better pray to your father, sea-god Poseidon." And all the Cyclopes marched grumpily home to their own caves.

The pole hissed like a red-hot poker stuck in a bucket of water.

Mastodon skull
The discovery of the skulls of mastodons – extinct, elephantlike animals – helped fuel the legend of the Cyclopes. People thought the large hole in the skull, where the trunk would have been, was a huge, central eye.

Poseidon
Polyphemus has a powerful ally to call upon in his hour of darkness – his father, Poseidon, god of the sea. In Greek myths, Poseidon is quick to take offense. Odysseus and his crew could hardly have a worse enemy.

Odysseus and his men were still trapped in the cave. They could dodge the blinded giant for a time, but how could they escape?

They watched Polyphemus crouch beside the entrance. He opened his wheel-door a little way to let out his flocks, feeling their woolly backs to make sure no man rode on them or ran beside them. That night, Odysseus lay thinking. Toward dawn, as the giant slept, Odysseus bound the sheep together in threes and tied his men underneath them.

He seized the biggest and strongest ram, and hung onto the fleece under its belly. Everyone waited.

When the giant finally shepherded his flock out of the cave, he couldn't know that his prisoners were riding to freedom. Down in the meadows Odysseus unfastened his friends. They quickly drove the flock downhill and onto their ship.

As the oars pulled the ship away from the land of the Cyclopes, Odysseus stood on its prow and shouted back at the wounded giant.

"Hey, Polyphemus! That'll teach you to entertain your strangers instead of eating them. Zeus has taken his revenge for your cruel insults!"

The Cyclops pulled a huge
rock from the ground.

High on a hill overlooking
the ship, Polyphemus shook with rage.
He pulled a huge rock from the ground and
hurled it in the direction of Odysseus's voice. It hit
the sea only a few feet from the ship, causing a great wave
that rocked the whole fleet.

Odysseus laughed and shouted again: "Cyclops, you missed us!
Now listen – if anyone ever asks who blinded you, tell them your
ugly eye was put out by Odysseus of Ithaca."

Then the Cyclops called upon his father, Poseidon, god of the sea,
for revenge. He lifted his hands and prayed at the top of his voice:
"Father Poseidon, god of ocean and earthquake, your son prays
Odysseus never reach his home in Ithaca. But if he do come home,
if he must come home, make it not for long time, make it all
unhappy, with all his shipmates dead and trouble in his own home."

That is how Polyphemus prayed in his pain. Odysseus and his
crew heard those words and shuddered. And the sea-god
Poseidon also heard. And he raised his great trident and
swore to answer the prayer of his blinded son.

Tales of the sea
*Being a seafaring people,
tales of the sea often feature
in Greek culture. This vase
painting depicts a story in
which Dionysus, the god
of wine, turns a band of
pirates into dolphins.*

—————— 🐟 ——————

The sin of pride
*There is no doubting
Odysseus's cunning as a
leader, but he does have one
weakness: pride. While
taunting Polyphemus he
boastfully reveals his true
name – a critical mistake.*

Chapter four

THE ISLE OF WINDS

The North, South, and East winds raged into a mighty tempest.

ODYSSEUS AND HIS MEN sailed onward, till they saw the floating island of Aeolia. All around the island stood a wall of bronze, shining hotly in the sun.

Here lived Aeolus, who had been appointed king of the winds by Zeus. He greeted Odysseus kindly, and he, his wife, and their six sons and six daughters entertained Odysseus and his crew with feasts and music for a whole month.

When it was time to journey onward, Odysseus asked a favor of the king: "We need the West Wind to blow us home to Ithaca," he said. "Would you stop the other winds from blowing us off course?"

"I'm happy to oblige," said the king of the winds. He took a great leather bag, made from the skin of an enormous ox. Then he whistled and the winds of the North, South, and East flew to him like so many tame pigeons.

The King took those winds, stuffed them in the great bag and secured the top of the bag with silver wire. Then he called the West Wind, which settled on his fist like a tame dove.

"Good West Wind," said Aeolus, "Carry brave Odysseus and his shipmates safely home to Ithaca."

So the fleet set sail again. After ten days, running before that kindly wind, they were close enough to

eir homeland, Ithaca, to see people sitting by fires on the shore.

Nearly home! Odysseus, happy in his heart, fell asleep on the
eck of his ship. But his crew were not so happy. They believed
at great leather bag was full of precious treasure.

"What a fine captain we've got," whispered one sailor to his
mpanions. "The king of the winds gives him a sackful of gold
d silver. All he lets us take home are a few mangy sheep."

"Let's open the bag," said another.

Carefully they unwound the silver wire. The North, South, and
ast winds burst out from the bag, circled in a whirlwind and raged
to a mighty tempest.

The ships were hurled across the sea, and Odysseus woke to the
ght of his homeland, Ithaca, disappearing into the distance.

His whole fleet was blown, like red leaves in autumn, back to the
land of Aeolia.

"I gave you everything a man could possibly need," the king of the
inds shouted.

You threw it all away. You must be the unluckiest man on earth.
s obvious that the gods hate you. Leave my island at once!"

So Odysseus and his men resumed their journey,
boring with their long oars, for there was
w no wind to help them.

What's in that bag?
*The crew's interest in the bag
Odysseus is given is
understandable. The sailors'
only payment for their toil
was a share of any booty
captured on the voyage.
But, as so often in Greek
myths, disobedience and
curiosity bring dire
consequences.*

Chapter five

CANNIBAL ISLAND

People eaters
Cannibalism – humans eating humans – was viewed with horror by the Greeks. They saw it as the ultimate crime against humanity.

Land of cannibals
King Antiphates is king of the Lestrigons, a tribe of cannibal giants. Some legends say they once lived in Sicily, others that Corsica was their home.

THE FLEET OF TWELVE SHIPS traveled gloomily onward until they came to a land in the far north. Here they found a natural harbor, a ring of high cliffs which could only be entered by a narrow channel. Eleven of the ships sailed in and tied up in the sheltered waters.

But Odysseus moored his ship just outside the cove. Then he sent three men to investigate the land.

Beside a bubbling spring they met a tall young woman fetching water. They asked her who the king of that country might be. She pointed to a nearby house.

"My father is the good King Antiphates," she said, " Come with me and he'll welcome you warmly."

They followed her cheerfully. But when her father appeared to greet them they saw that Antiphates was a cannibal giant with blood smeared all over his beard.

He gave a squealing laugh, pounced on one of the three men and began to eat him alive. The other two ran back to the ships.

But King Antiphates stamped through his village, calling out his fellow cannibals: "Hunt down the foreigners! Tonight we feast!"

A crowd of greedy giants swarmed over the cliffs around the harbor. Standing either side of the channel leading to the open sea,

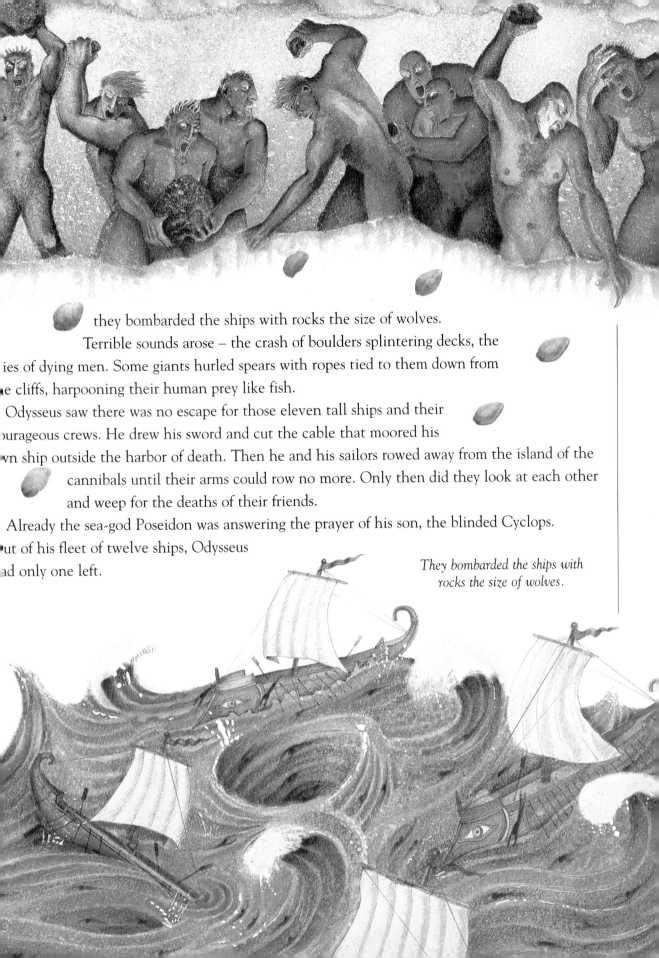

they bombarded the ships with rocks the size of wolves.

Terrible sounds arose – the crash of boulders splintering decks, the
ies of dying men. Some giants hurled spears with ropes tied to them down from
e cliffs, harpooning their human prey like fish.

Odysseus saw there was no escape for those eleven tall ships and their
ourageous crews. He drew his sword and cut the cable that moored his
vn ship outside the harbor of death. Then he and his sailors rowed away from the island of the
cannibals until their arms could row no more. Only then did they look at each other
and weep for the deaths of their friends.

Already the sea-god Poseidon was answering the prayer of his son, the blinded Cyclops.
ut of his fleet of twelve ships, Odysseus
ad only one left.

They bombarded the ships with rocks the size of wolves.

Chapter six

CIRCE

THE LONE SHIP SAILED on and on, until it came to the island of Aeaea. Odysseus and his men collapsed on a golden beach. There they lay, sad and exhausted, for two days and nights.

On the third morning Odysseus climbed a small mountain. From there he could see surf beating all around the green island. Then he saw signs of life – a gray spiral of smoke rising from the heart of a wood.

Odysseus was in a cautious mood – he'd met too many man-eating giants lately. He went back to his crew and ordered the noble Eurylochus to take half the company – twenty-two men – and find out who lived in that forest.

Eurylochus and his men followed a winding path through the trees until they came to a tall castle of white stone standing in a clearing.

Prowling all around the house were mountain wolves and lions. The sailors turned to run, but the wolves and lions wagged their tails and rubbed up against the men's legs like tame cats and puppies. For these were not wild animals, but men who had been transformed by magic spells and potions.

From inside the castle came the sound of a silvery voice singing. One of the men called out. The ivory door of the castle opened slowly. There stood a woman. She was as beautiful as a goddess, and her shining gown was studded with jewels of ever-changing colors.

"I am Circe," she said with a smile. "Welcome to my castle."

The men eagerly followed her inside. Only Eurylochus, suspecting a trick, held back and watched through a window.

He saw Circe and her maidens prepare a meal of cheese and

The Enchantress
Circe is not a goddess, but a mortal with magical powers similar to those of a witch in a fairy tale. Like a witch she is a lonely, isolated figure, yet she is not old and ugly (like most witches) but beautiful and alluring.

Drinking cup
Odysseus's men could have drunk out of pottery cups like this one. It dates from 1650 BC, the time of the Mycenean civilization in Greece. The cup has links with the sea, too – a cuttlefish is painted on it.

*Circe raised her wand
and struck each
of the men.*

barley and golden honey.

He watched as the crew gobbled it down greedily.

Then they gulped down all the wine she offered them
and shouted for more. "I shall give you even more than you
ask for," said Circe sweetly. "For you have behaved like pigs in
my castle."

She raised her wand and struck each of the men. And they
were instantly changed into twenty-two hogs – with bristles all
over and wet pink snouts.

Circe laughed and drove them out of her castle to grunt and
snuffle for acorns in the mud. Eurylochus ran back to Odysseus
and blurted out the news: "The men have been turned into pigs!"

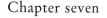

Chapter seven

THE ENCHANTED ENCHANTRESS

ODYSSEUS PICKED UP his sword and marched angrily through the wood. But on the winding path he met Hermes, the messenger of the gods and the friend of all travelers, disguised as a young man.

"Poor Odysseus," said Hermes. "The goddess Athene, who watches over your troubled life, sent me to help you. I'll show you how to free your friends from the enchantress." Hermes plucked a milk-white flower with a black root from the ground.

"This herb is called moly," he said. "Eat it, and Circe's magic wine will have no power over you. You may draw your sword and force her to free your men."

Hermes plucked a milk-white flower from the ground.

Odysseus thanked Hermes, and walked on, chewing the magic moly. At the castle, Circe greeted him, seated him, gave him magic wine to drink and watched him carefully.

But Odysseus did not change into a boar, as she had planned. He remained a man, a strong, angry man who stared back at her. "Witch!" he shouted. "You changed my men into pigs. Change them back or I'll run you through with my good sword."

So Circe went out and touched each of the pigs with her wand.

And their bristles dropped out and they stood on two feet and they were men again, but all of them younger and more handsome than ever before.

And now Circe seemed to be enchanted by Odysseus. And he enjoyed the company of the lovely Circe. She invited him and all his men to come and live in her wonderful castle. And there they stayed, feasting with her and her handmaidens.

Meanwhile, back in Ithaca, their families had not forgotten them. Penelope, the wife of Odysseus, was troubled. Ever since the fall of Troy there had been rumors that Odysseus had been killed in battle or drowned or eaten by giants.

More and more men, young and old, crowded into her house demanding to marry her and refusing to leave until she chose one of them. Penelope and her young son Telemachus were powerless to drive out these suitors.

So they ate her food and drank her wine and pestered her every evening with the question: "Which one of us will you marry?"

Finally she told them: "I'm too busy to think of marriage until I have finished weaving a shroud for Laertes, the father of Odysseus. When that is finished, I shall make up my mind."

But deep in her heart, Penelope believed that Odysseus was still alive. So every day she wove some more of the shroud. And every night she unpicked all she had woven during the day. Penelope would resist as long as she possibly could.

Penelope
Odysseus's loyal wife buys time for herself by weaving a shroud, a cloth used for wrapping a dead body.

Penelope and Telemachus were powerless to drive out the suitors.

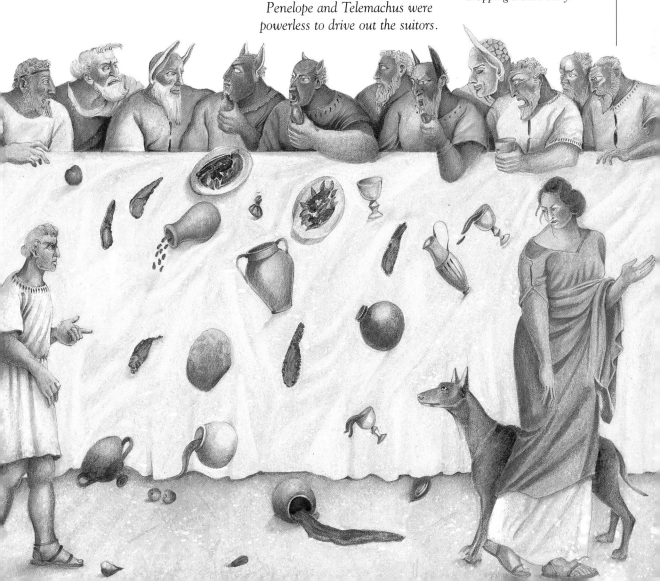

THE GODS' REALMS

The Greeks believed the world was divided into realms, each ruled by a god.

Mount Olympus, home of the immortal gods

The Earth, home of mortal men

The Oceanus River, which encircled the Earth

The Land of the Dead

The Styx River

Hades, the Underworld

GODS AND GODDESSES

THE ANCIENT GREEKS developed a wonderfully detailed pantheon of gods and goddesses, most of whom lived on Mount Olympus. There was a god or goddess for every aspect of nature and every human activity or quality. Only a few of these immortal beings, however, feature in the Trojan War (see pp. 8–9) and *The Odyssey*.

Helios

To bring light to the world, the sun god drives his chariot across the sky each day, descending into the great sea called Ocean at night. Odysseus's men incur the god's anger when they eat his cattle.

Laurence Olivier as Zeus in the 198[] film Clash of the Titans

Zeus

Watching from Mount Olympus, the king of the gods does not take sides durin[] the Trojan War. He destroys Odysseus's ship with a thunderbolt as a favor to Helios.

Bronze statue of Poseidon, 450 BC

Hermes

The quick-witted messenger of the gods and a son of Zeus, Hermes has a magical winged helmet and sandals. He is a supporter of Odysseus, with whom he shares many character traits.

Athene

The goddess of wisdom, Athene backed the Greeks during the war with Troy, and helps Odysseus win back his kingdom from the suitors.

Athene by Mantegna Andrea, 15th century

Poseidon

The god of the sea, Zeus's brother Poseidon does everything in his power to prevent Odysseus returning home, in revenge for the blinding of his son, the cyclops Polyphemus.

Aphrodite

The goddess of love helped cause the Trojan War by encouraging Paris to steal Helen away from her husband, Menelaus. She protected Paris in battle, but could not prevent his death and the destruction of Troy.

Hades

The third brother of Zeus is king of the Underworld, also called Hades. This disma[] place has one hot area, Tartarus, where ev[] souls suffer, and one beautiful spot, Elysiu[] where the ghosts of heroes dwell. Hades lie[] underground, but can be reached by journeying, like Odysseus, beyond the Oceanus River.

Charon

An immortal being, but not a god, Charon ferried dead souls over the Styx River to the Underworld. The Trojan War kept Charon very busy.

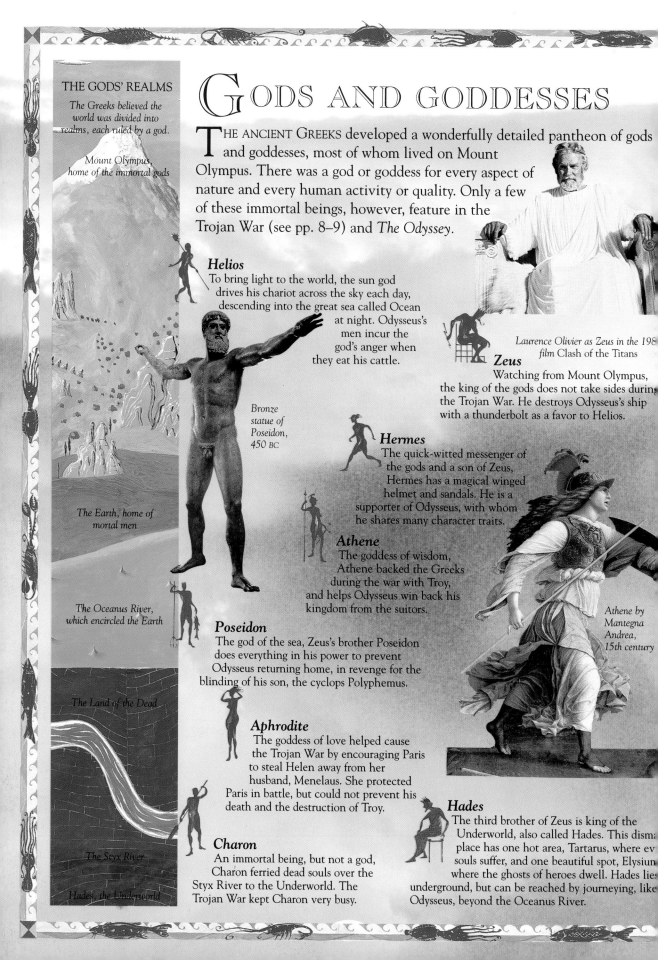

Religious festival

This wine bowl (below) shows a boisterous procession of worshipers of Athene. Some are playing musical instruments, one holds a jar of wine, and another leads a bull to sacrifice to the goddess.

The birth of Athene

tories of the gods often ppear in Greek art. This etail from a cup shows thene, goddess of wisdom, pringing from the head of eus, her father – set free by an ax-blow from laephaestus, god of fire nd metalwork.

WORSHIPPING THE GODS

Religion was central to Greek life: festivals dedicated to the gods were were held throughout the year, magnificent temples were built in their honor, and the people uttered prayers and made sacrifices of animals, food, wine, and valuable objects in the hope of winning special favors.

Athene Reveals
Ithaca to Ulysses,
*by Giuseppe Bottani
Mantua, 18th century.*

Temple of Poseidon, Sounion, Greece

Places of worship

Magnificent temples honored certain gods and displayed the power and prosperity of a city or region. They were built of limestone or marble, decorated with statues and friezes, and had ceilings of wood.

The gods on Earth

People believed the gods were closely involved in their lives. They communicated with them through priests, who also relayed the gods' will. Animals' behavior or natural phenomena – storms, winds etc – were taken as signs from the gods. Many legends told of gods appearing to human beings and advising, punishing, or even falling in love with them.

Chapter eight

THE LAND OF THE DEAD

Sacrificial lamb
Sacrificing animals to gain
favor from the gods was
common to many cultures.
Black sheep could have been
chosen because black is a
color associated with death.

FTER A YEAR in Circe's magical castle, the Greeks were anxious to sail for home. "That's not so easy," Circe told Odysseus as they sat feasting on roast peacocks and honeycakes. "Poseidon hates you. If you are to avoid his revenge, you must seek advice. Sail to the shores of a river called Ocean.

"Leave your ship there and boldly walk into the Land of the Dead. And there, between the River of Flames and the River of Tears, make a blood-sacrifice.

"This will raise the ghost of the ancient prophet Teiresias. Let the noble ghost take a drink of blood and he may tell you how you can travel home to Ithaca."

The next morning Odysseus roused his men and they prepared to sail. They hurried aboard their ship, taking a black ram and a black ewe for the sacrifice. Circe raised her wand and the North Wind filled their sails. They sailed until they came to the edge of the world and the thick darkness of the river called Ocean. They left their ship and walked, in terror, into the Land of the Dead.

Between the River of Flames and the River of Tears they dug a
long trench. They scattered its banks with sweet milk, yellow wine,
and fresh water, then sprinkled these with white barley.

Odysseus, as he had been told by Circe, took the black ram and
the black ewe and cut their throats as a sacrifice. Their rich blood
flowed and filled the trench. Odysseus sat down with his sword on
guard so that no ghost could come and taste the blood before the
prophet Teiresias.

At last the ghost of Teiresias himself appeared, like a tall, white,
shaking tree. Odysseus allowed the great prophet to drink blood
from the trench, only then would he be be able to speak.

As the crimson blood trickled down through his beard, Teiresias
spoke, in the chanting voice of a true prophet: "Odysseus, your
homeward journey will be hard and dangerous. The sea-god
Poseidon hates you for blinding his darling son.

"You and your friends may yet reach Ithaca. But beware. Avoid
the Island of the Sun God, whose eyes see everything. If you do
land there, remember that it is death to touch his sacred cattle."

*The rich blood flowed and filled
the trench.*

Eyesight to the blind
*Teiresias, was struck blind
by the goddess Athene when
he glimpsed her bathing. She
was sorry afterward, but
could not undo what had
been done, so she gave him
the gift of prophecy.*

The ghost of the prophet continued his warnings to Odysseus: "If you ever do reach your home, you will find it full of troubles. Solve these, and one more journey still lies ahead of you.

"You must travel inland with a long oar on your shoulder. Walk alone till you find people who have never seen or heard of the sea. Then plant your oar in the earth and make a rich sacrifice to Lord Poseidon. Only then may the sea god and master of the earthquake forgive your crime."

Teiresias faded from sight like smoke into the sky. When the next ghost approached, Odysseus nearly dropped his sword into the trench of blood. For there stood the spirit of his own mother, Anticleia.

Odysseus stood and cried out: "Mother! Nobody told me you were dead. Were you killed? Or did some plague carry you off?"

"No one killed me and I caught no disease," his mother answered. "It was the hurting in my heart whenever I thought of you, my wise and gentle Odysseus, it was that hurting which ended my life. But your father, good Laertes, is still alive."

Three times Odysseus, the hot tears blinding him, tried to take his mother in his arms. Three times, like a beloved shadow, she slipped through his arms. She vanished away like river-mist in the morning.

Ten ghosts took her place, and then a hundred and then a thousand crowding around – men, women, children, and babies. There were kings and priests and warriors and merchants and beggars and slaves, tens of thousands of them now, filling the air with moans and curses and questions. Odysseus panicked. He turned and ran back, through a fog of wailing ghosts, to the safety of his ship. The crew struck out with their long oars toward the island of Circe.

At her castle, Circe greeted them all like heroes. In the past year she had come to love Odysseus. So she warned him of dangers still to come, and secret ways in which he might avert them. Then Circe and Odysseus said a sad farewell.

As the ship set sail, Circe wandered alone along the winding path through the woods to her castle, singing a magic song to help Odysseus on his way and patting the heads of her pet wolves and lions absentmindedly.

Ghosts crowded around, filling the air with moans and curses and questions.

Chapter nine

The Sirens

THE GOOD SHIP glided across a calm gray sea toward an island of sloping meadows, golden in the sun. The crew were all for landing, but Odysseus knew better.

"That is the Island of the Sirens," he told them. "Circe warned me to steer clear of it. For the Sirens are beautiful but deadly.

"They sit beside the ocean combing their long golden hair and singing to passing sailors. But anyone who hears their song is bewitched by its sweetness, and they are drawn to that island like iron to a magnet. And their ship smashes upon rocks as sharp as spears. And those sailors join the many victims of the Sirens in a meadow full of skeletons."

Odysseus took a large block of beeswax, a gift from Circe. He broke it into small pieces and gave one to each of his men, telling them to soften it and put it in their ears, so that they would not hear the song of the Sirens.

But he wanted to hear that famous song and survive. So he ordered his sailors to tie him firmly to the mast. When this had been done, and the beeswax earplugs were in place, the men rowed the ship alongside the island.

Then Odysseus heard the magical song of the Sirens as it floated over the summertime waters:

Artists' inspiration

The legend of the Sirens' beautiful singing and their treacherous, evil natures have inspired many artists, poets, and songwriters. Odysseus was not the first human to pass them. Jason also managed the feat, by asking the great harpist Orpheus to drown their voices with his own music. This 18th-century engraving shows the Sirens with scaly tales, like mermaids.

"Odysseus, bravest of heroes,
Draw near to us, on our green island,
Odysseus, we'll teach you wisdom,
We'll give you love, sweeter than honey.
The songs we sing, soothe away sorrow,
And in our arms, you will be happy.
Odysseus, bravest of heroes,
The songs we sing, will bring you peace."

Going for a song

The Sirens are half women, half birds. In some legends, the Sirens kill their victims; in others, those that hear their song are so entranced they die of hunger. Homer leaves their fate unclear, but some tales relate that the Sirens were so furious that Odysseus had heard their song and escaped that they drowned themselves.

This song enchanted the heart of Odysseus. He longed to plunge into the waves, swim to the island, and embrace the Sirens. He strained against his bonds till they cut deep into the flesh of his arms and back. He nodded and scowled at his earplugged men, urging them to free him. But they only pulled more and more strongly on the oars.

To Odysseus, bewitched by the song, the Sirens looked as beautiful as Helen of Troy. But to his deaf crew they seemed like hungry monsters with vicious, crooked claws.

The ship sped forward and soon the song of the Sirens was an echo of an echo. It was only then that the crew stopped rowing and unplugged their ears. Eurylochus unbound his grateful captain, who had now come to his senses. And already Odysseus could see more danger ahead – a dazzling cloud of spray and fierce waves clashing between two tall cliffs.

He ordered his sailors to tie him firmly to the mast.

Chapter ten

SCYLLA AND CHARYBDIS

NOW THE SHIP had to sail between two cliffs, where white water raged like a mountain torrent. That looked dangerou enough to the crew. But only Odysseus knew the real dangers, thanks to Circe.

On the left-hand side of the narrows gaped the terrible whirlpool Charybdis. And in a high cave on the right-hand cliff dwelled a six-headed monster named Scylla. Each of her snakelike heads swung from a long and scaly neck. It was her delight to snatch sailors off the decks of their ships with her long pointed teeth or with her twelve long tentacles.

Steer the ship to the left and be swallowed down by Charybdis? Or steer to the right and be devoured by Scylla?

Odysseus knew he had little time to decide. Strapping on his armor and seizing two long spears, he took his stand on the prow of the ship. Then, with all the confidence he could muster, he ordered his men to steer along the right-hand cliff.

They obeyed gladly, for while they could plainly see the foam churning around the whirlpool's mouth, they had never heard of Scylla, the dreadful monster who lurked in her cave, listening out for the splash of approaching oars.

While the sailors stared in terror at the wild circling of the whirlpool's throat, the six heads of Scylla sprang from her dark cave. Six of the crew were seized and hauled up into the air,

Monstrous curse
Scylla had once been a beautiful girl. However she offended the sorceress Circe, who changed her into a hideous monster.

creaming for their captain to save them. But their cries were soon crushed by the monster's
aws. The ship shot through the straits and into the open sea.

Odysseus and his crew wept at the loss of their comrades, their only comfort the bitter
hought that they would all have been drowned had they sought to pass by Charybdis.

It was not long before the survivors reached the island where Helios the sun god kept
is sacred herd of cattle. Odysseus told his sailors: "Teiresias, the great prophet, warned me
o avoid this island."

But Eurylochus was angry and said: "We all know you're a man of
ron, captain – but we're flesh and blood. We're dying of hunger and we
eed a rest."

The whole crew cheered him and Odysseus had to give in. But he
nade them all swear not to touch any of the sun god's cattle.

That night there was a great storm and Odysseus went ashore alone,
p into the mountains to pray to the gods for help.
Meanwhile Eurylochus and the hungry crew
anded, killed two of the sacred cattle,
oasted them, and feasted on the beach.

Six of the crew were seized, but their
cries were soon crushed by the
monster's jaws.

Helios, the sun god, blazed with anger. He shouted: "Great Zeus, these sailors have killed and eaten my holy cattle. Punish them, or I'll go down to Hades and shine only for the dead."

Zeus smiled: "Stay in the blue sky, sun god. I'll smash their ship to atoms."

He raised one finger. A wind like an ax chopped through the base of the ship's mast. It fell like a great tree.

Zeus hurled his thunderbolt. The ship's back broke. Its crew sank like a handful of pebbles.

Only Odysseus survived. He balanced on a single plank as the crippled ship was dragged by raging currents toward Charybdis, the terrible whirlpool.

Suddenly a wave flung him high into the air. He reached out and grabbed – something. He found himself hanging onto the bending branch of a fig tree above the whirlpool.

Zeus smiled: "I'll smash their ship to atoms."

The mouth of the whirlpool spat out the ship's mast.

He clung on like a bat. Looking down he could see Charybdis, a ghastly, green throat longing to swallow him down.

He gasped in the terror of death.

His muscles were burning, the branch was bending. But then the mouth of the whirlpool spat out the ship's mast.

It shot upward like a spear. Odysseus tracked its flight, then leapt onto the mast as it fell back into the sea, well clear of the whirlpool's deadly spiral.

He climbed astride the mast and looked around.

All his friends were gone. Sighing deeply, he paddled with his strong plowman's hands, away from danger, toward new perils.

Zeus

The king of the gods, the bringer of light, the ruler of the weather, the judge of all quarrels, Zeus is depicted here holding a thunderbolt and seated in a chariot drawn by eagles.

Fantasy island
Legends say that the Mediterranean island of Gozo, near Malta, was once Calypso's island, which Homer names Ogygia.

Lonely nymph
Calypso is a demi-goddess, the daughter of Atlas, a giant who holds up the heavens. Homer calls her "the nymph of the lovely locks." He also describes her as having a beautiful singing voice.

Chapter eleven

Calypso's Island

THE SHIP'S MAST ROCKED over the waves like a wild horse galloping over rolling hills. Odysseus clung on, gasping for breath. A great wave caught the mast and dragged it for a mile before hurling it up onto an island of sweet-smelling forests and glowing flowers.

There lay Odysseus, face down on the sand. He felt empty, lost and lonely, like a ghost on its first day. There he was found by Calypso, the kind and beautiful goddess who lived in a marvelous cave on the island.

She took him to her magic home and nursed him back to health. She fed him, sang to him, and loved him. But whenever he spoke of returning home, her eyes became like two cold diamonds and he was afraid.

So he stayed with Calypso on her island for seven long years.

She was very happy. But all the time Odysseus longed to see the smoke rising from his home in Ithaca, and he grew sad and silent.

The goddess Athene pitied him and persuaded Zeus to send Hermes, messenger of the gods, to speak to Calypso. Hermes bound on his golden sandals with wings at the heels and flew down from Mount Olympus.

He swooped down upon the sea and skimmed across the waves like a cormorant hunting down fishes. He reached the island of Calypso and walked to the great cavern where the goddess lived.

The mouth of the cave was sheltered by aspen trees and cypresses. Many birds nested in those trees, horned owls and falcons and talkative seabirds. Vines clustered around the cave mouth, heavy with purple grapes. From a scarlet fire floated the perfume of logs of juniper and cedar.

Calypso invited Hermes to sit in a shining chair and gave him a golden bowl of ambrosia, the food of the gods, to eat and a silver goblet of red nectar to drink.

Then he explained his mission: "Calypso, my father Zeus says you have a man here who's been really unlucky. He fought for ten years in the Trojan War. And on his way home he's lost all of his shipmates. It's time he was allowed to go home to Ithaca."

As Calypso listened she began to tremble with fear and anger.

"How cruel and jealous you gods are!" she cried. "You can't bear to see a goddess living happily with a mortal man. I saved him, I nursed him, I even hoped to make him immortal like me." She sighed. "But I suppose nobody can disobey the great Zeus."

Hermes nodded. "Good. Send him home now. Or Zeus will be displeased."

Hermes left quickly, not wishing to see the tears of Calypso.

Hermes skimmed across the waves like a cormorant hunting down fishes.

Ambrosia

In Greek myths, ambrosia is the food of the gods, the favorite delicacy of the immortals of Olympus. "Ambrosia" is also the name given to a mixture of pollen and nectar that worker bees feed to bee grubs. Another name for it is "beebread."

Forever young

Calypso, like all the Greek gods, is immortal – she can live forever without growing old. Odysseus and Penelope are humans – mortals – and so age as the years go by.

Cypress trees

One of the most common trees in the Mediterranean region, the cypress can often be seen growing in groves. Tall and straight, this conifer would be good for raft building.

Trident

A three-pronged spear formerly used by Greek fisherman, the trident is always associated with the god Poseidon, who often used it to stir up terrible storms.

Calypso walked slowly down to the sea and came upon Odysseus sitting on the sand, staring across the wine-dark waters toward Ithaca. She put her hand on his shoulder.

"My sad friend," she said, "It is time for you to leave my island. If you make a raft, I will stock it with food and drink and send you a following wind to carry you home."

Odysseus was suspicious. "Sweet goddess," he said. "Do you promise that this isn't some trick to keep me here?"

Calypso smiled at him and patted his brown cheek with her hand. "Odysseus, not everyone's a crafty old trickster like you. I'm letting you go because I'm sorry for you. But tell me, this Penelope, this wife you're so anxious to see, is she as beautiful as I am?"

It is dangerous to offend a goddess. Odysseus thought quickly before replying. "Your youthful loveliness can never fade, Calypso," he said. "Penelope is a mere mortal. But I have a man's longing for his own home."

Next day Calypso gave Odysseus a bronze ax. He cut down twenty trees and began to make his raft. After five days of work, he dragged his raft on rollers and launched it on a peaceful sea. Calypso presented him with a sweet-smelling cloak and tunic and waved goodbye as the raft sailed gently away into the distance.

For seventeen days Odysseus sailed. On the eighteenth, he saw an island crowned with snowy peaks.

But Poseidon the Sea God saw the frail raft and remembered how Odysseus had blinded his son, Polyphemus the Cyclops.

So he raised his trident, bringing down all four winds in a swirling dark storm. A wave arose like a green glass mountain. It curled above Odysseus and then crashed down, smashing his raft and throwing him into the surging sea.

Odysseus desperately swam under water, weighed down by waterlogged clothes. With bursting lungs, he dragged his clothes off and fought his way to the surface. He grabbed and caught the raft's broken deck and clung on desperately. After three days and nights, a great wave carried him and threw him onto a beach.

Along the sands he staggered till he came to a fresh stream. There he drank deeply. He found some soft earth among green bushes, scraped himself a hollow and covered himself with a thick blanket of dead leaves. And then, in this hero's nest, he closed his eyes in a long, deep sleep.

A wave arose like a green glass mountain.

Axhead
This Greek bronze axhead would have been attached to a wooden shaft. A pointed ax like this was probably more use as a weapon than for cutting down trees.

Fun and games
The Greeks enjoyed playing games, and, as Nausicaa and her maids demonstrate, girls took part as well as boys. This relief shows some young men playing what looks like an early form of hockey.

Odysseus was a wild sight.

Chapter twelve

Nausicaa

THE NAKED ODYSSEUS slept under his pile of leaves on a beach in the unknown land of Phaeacia. Meanwhile the beautiful Princess Nausicaa and her handmaidens were playing ball nearby.

One of Nausicaa's throws flew wide. The ball splashed into the river. All the women laughed and Odysseus awoke.

"What's this?" he asked himself. "The hunting cries of cannibals? Or kind and gentle people? I'd better find out."

He found a bough thick with leaves to hide his nakedness. He w[as] still a wild sight, his body encrusted with white sea-salt, his beard matted, his hair standing on end.

All the women except Nausicaa ran away. The Princess had bee[n] taught to fear no man. She stood her ground.

Odysseus spoke to her from a respectful distance: "I cannot tell if you are a goddess or a mortal woman. But listen to me mercifully. In the wars and in my travels I have suffered greatly. I have battled against bad luck and giants and monsters. I have lost all my friends.

"Please give me something to wear and let me have food and drink, for I am a stranger. And may the gods grant you every happiness your heart desires."

Nausicaa smiled and said: "Gentle stranger, welcome to the land of Phaeacia. I am the daughter of the good King Alcinous."

She handed him her long cloak to cover his nakedness and then Nausicaa and her handmaidens drove him back to the golden palace of King Alcinous.

The King gave a great feast for Odysseus in his beautiful palace gardens, among great bronze statues of dogs, and orange trees, and sparkling fountains and flowing streams, and a thousand sweet-smelling flowers.

King Alcinous sent fifty young men to prepare a ship for Odysseus. The next morning Nausicaa and her family waved goodbye as Odysseus sailed away in a ship driven by fifty Phaeacian oars, full speed across the wine-dark sea.

They landed by starlight in a bay on the coast of Ithaca. Odysseus was sleeping. The Phaeacian crew carried him gently ashore and laid him on the sand. Then they set sail for home. Odysseus, all alone, slept deeply under a moon like a newly minted silver coin.

Walled in

Poseidon took revenge upon the Phaeacians for helping Odysseus. The boat was wrecked on the way back from Ithaca. Poseidon then caused an earthquake, which surrounded the city of the Phaeacians with a wall of mountains. Never again would they be able to sail forth in their proud ships.

All the women except Nausicaa ran away.

Chapter thirteen

THE HOMECOMING

The noble beggar

This 18th-century painting shows the goddess Athene transforming Odysseus into an aged beggar. In this lowly disguise he will be able to discover who can be trusted in his kingdom, and who is selfish and cruel.

Gods in disguise

In Greek mythology, the gods often appear to mortals disguised as humble folk – shepherds, travelers, or beggars. This creates a magical atmosphere, in which ordinary things are not what they seem.

ODYSSEUS STRETCHED AND YAWNED and looked around. At first he thought he was in a cloud. But then he realized that the beach was covered with a deep mist, colored pink by the dawn.

Through the mist there moved toward him the tall figure of a young shepherd. The shepherd greeted Odysseus, but even as he spoke, his appearance changed and brightened until he was transformed into the beautiful, majestic goddess of wisdom.

Odysseus sprang to his feet: "Mighty Goddess Athene!" he said. "Please tell me where I am. Is this a friendly country or is it dangerous?"

"Both friendly and dangerous," said the goddess, "for it contains those you love most and those who hate you. This is the famous, rocky land of Ithaca."

Odysseus felt his heart jump in his chest. "Ithaca!" he shouted. "Home at last!"

He bowed his head. Athene raised her right hand. The mist scattered and now the brave traveler could see the hills of his own land, golden in the sunlight. He knelt down and kissed the earth. "What shall I do?" he asked.

Athene spoke: "You will find your house full of villains. For three years they have stayed there, pestering your noble wife Penelope, eating her food and drinking her wine. "They are all competing to marry Penelope. So far she has managed to put them off by saying that she will marry one of them

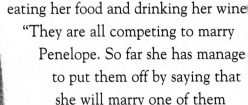

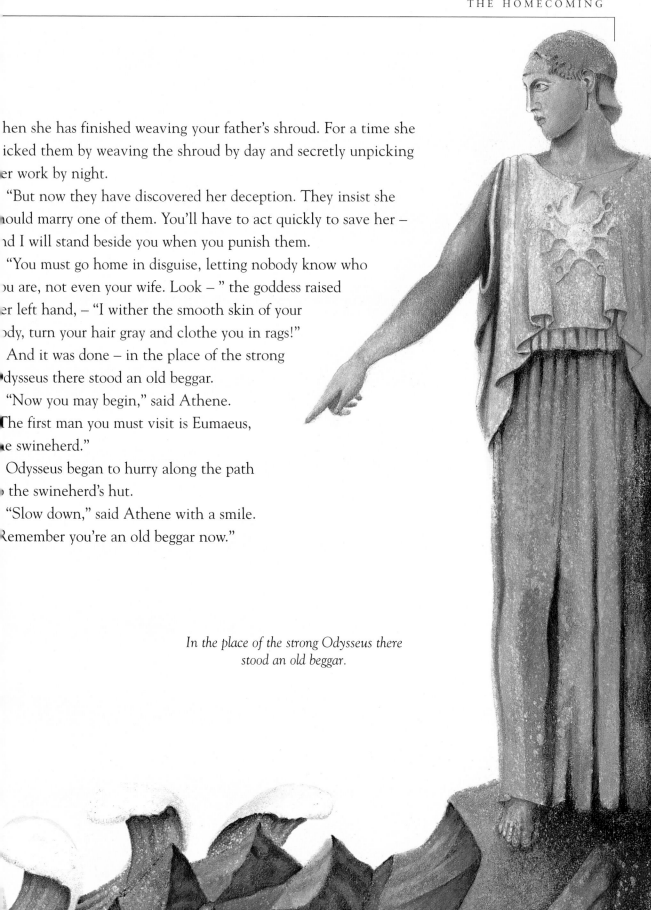

hen she has finished weaving your father's shroud. For a time she
icked them by weaving the shroud by day and secretly unpicking
er work by night.

"But now they have discovered her deception. They insist she
ould marry one of them. You'll have to act quickly to save her –
d I will stand beside you when you punish them.

"You must go home in disguise, letting nobody know who
u are, not even your wife. Look – " the goddess raised
er left hand, – "I wither the smooth skin of your
dy, turn your hair gray and clothe you in rags!"

And it was done – in the place of the strong
dysseus there stood an old beggar.

"Now you may begin," said Athene.
The first man you must visit is Eumaeus,
e swineherd."

Odysseus began to hurry along the path
the swineherd's hut.

"Slow down," said Athene with a smile.
Remember you're an old beggar now."

In the place of the strong Odysseus there
stood an old beggar.

Four fierce dogs rushed from behind the swineherd's hut. They charged the beggarlike Odysseus, barking and tearing at his rags with their yellow teeth. But the swineherd Eumaeus dropped the sandal he was mending, shouted and threw gravel at the dogs till they cowered away.

"Walk into my hut and share my bread and wine," said Eumaeus. "For my old master always said that strangers and beggars should be honored as the children of Zeus."

"Who is your old master?" asked Odysseus.

"He was Odysseus, the best of masters and the kindest of men," said Eumaeus. "But he is long lost and dead and gone."

Odysseus put his hand on the swineherd's shaking shoulder. "Do not weep," he said. "For I swear Odysseus will come home."

At this moment a tall young man walked into the hut.

Odysseus stared and stared. The young man nodded to him and said to the swineherd: "Eumaeus, where does this guest of yours come from?"

"From far across the seas," said Eumaeus. "Please sit with him, for I must go and feed the pigs." He lumbered out of the hut.

Athene chose that moment to whisper in the ear of Odysseus:

"This is your son Telemachus – tell him who you are. Then you can make your plans together."

"I am your father Odysseus," said the hero. "Athene has disguised my body so that I look like a beggar. But I am the man, home at last after so many years of war, bad luck, and wandering."

The faithful swineherd
Epic stories such as The Odyssey, *were so popular that scenes from them often decorated Greek household utensils. This vase from the 5th century* BC *shows Odysseus meeting Eumaeus the swineherd.*

50

Telemachus walked back to his home feeling happier and stronger than ever before.

Telemachus flung his arms around his father. Both of them broke down and cried. It was a long time before they began to plan their revenge on the suitors.

"Walk home ahead of me, but don't tell your mother I am back," said Odysseus. "I will arrive later, still disguised as a beggar. Those suitors may insult me, but don't you intervene.

"Athene will tell me when the time has come to strike. Then I will nod to you. But first you must take all the suitors' weapons from the great hall and lock them away."

They agreed every detail of the battle to come – then Telemachus walked back to his home, feeling happier and stronger than ever before. Some way behind him a ragged beggar stumbled along with a small green bird perched on his shoulder. Or perhaps it was Odysseus, accompanied by Athene.

Bird of Athene
Sacred to Athene, the owl was the emblem of the city of Athens, and appeared on many coins. If an owl entered a house it was thought death would follow.

Odysseus hobbled up the steps to the hall.

Oil container

Kindness to strangers
Penelope is doing the poor stranger a great honor by lending him her husband's clothes and instructing Eurycleia to rub his body with oil. Her hospitality indicates what a good, generous person she is.

Chapter fourteen

ODYSSEUS'S REVENGE

THE OLD BEGGAR stood and stared at the stone steps leading up to the great hall of the house of Odysseus. Down in the dust, in the shadow of the steps, an old dog pricked up his ears and raised his head.

An old dog called Argus, he had been a puppy when he last saw Odysseus nineteen years ago. Now he was old and blind and his coat was full of fleas, but Argus recognized the scent of his master. He wagged his tail feebly and dropped his ears, but he was not strong enough to stand. Odysseus knelt beside his good old dog.

He took Argus in his arms, fleas and all.

That old dog licked the salt of his master's cheek. His loyal heart filled with happiness and he died. Odysseus remembered he must pretend to be a beggar. He gently laid his old dog's corpse in the cool shadows, to be buried later, and hobbled up the steps into the hubbub of the hall.

The great hall was full of drunken suitors, eating like wolves, singing like crows, and dancing like ducks. They shouted for more wine and hit the servants who brought it. They threw food at each other, fell over benches, vomited, and laughed like hyenas. When the beggar asked for scraps from the table they sneered at him and

one of them, Antinous, threw a wooden stool which hit Odysseus hard on the shoulder.

When Penelope heard that a beggar from over the seas was in the hall, she sent for him. Any stranger might have news of her husband. Odysseus was brought to her, but she did not recognize him. And he was strangely silent, for he hardly trusted himself to speak without revealing his identity.

It had been twenty years since he last saw her. But Penelope's beauty was still as clear and warm and shining, her voice was still a music which went straight to his heart.

Penelope called her old nurse, Eurycleia, to bathe the beggar and rub him down with olive oil, and give him some of her husband's clothes to wear. The old woman fetched a basin and began to bathe him. But as she washed his legs she recognized a scar on his leg where a tusk had wounded the young Odysseus during a boar-hunt.

She ran her hand over this scar, burst into tears and said: "You are Odysseus, my little boy!"

"Shh," said Odysseus. "Nobody must know, or we'll both be killed. Not a word, sweet nurse." And he kissed her and she smiled and put a finger to her lips. Then she dried him and wrapped him in a towel just as she did when he was four years old.

The great hall was full of drunken suitors.

Rich man's sport
Hunting was popular among the wealthier Greeks. Odysseus would have relished pitting his wits and skill with bow and spear against a dangerous animal such as a boar, whose tusks can inflict serious injuries.

Straight shooter
In the Greek army, archers were generally drawn from the poorer folk; the sons of the wealthy fought with expensive shields and spears. Yet Odysseus's great bow is no humble weapon, but a symbol of his strength and prowess as a warrior – talents that he has been unable to rely on in his adventures up to this point.

Hall interior
This depiction of the Palace of Minos at Knossos, Crete, with its fine dolphin fresco conveys a sense of the Greek aristocracy's taste in furniture and decoration.

When Odysseus was dressed, he was taken by his old nurse to speak with Penelope again. Penelope still did not recognize him, but she liked him and trusted him.

"I can't put off those suitors any longer," she said. "Now they've seen through my weaving trick they've sworn to draw lots for my hand. But I am Penelope – not a lottery prize!

"I have suggested a trial of skill and strength. Whoever can string the great bow of Odysseus and shoot an arrow through the rings in a row of twelve axheads – as my husband used to do – that man shall carry me off as his bride."

Odysseus smiled and said: "Good lady, hold your contest as soon as possible. Cunning old Odysseus will be here long before those weaklings can string his bow."

That same night the contest was staged. Telemachus placed the twelve axes in a row down the great hall while the suitors feasted. Meanwhile Odysseus took Eumaeus and his cowherd aside, revealed his identity and recruited them for the battle to come.

Penelope entered the hall, her long arms full of the mighty bow and a quiver of deadly arrows. The suitors fell silent as she announced: "If any of you can string this bow and shoot through twelve axheads I will go with him, leaving this house which I love so much. Eumaeus – take the bow."

She left the hall and the swineherd took charge of proceedings. First the magician Leodes took the bow, but his pale hands were too weak to bend it.

Next came big Eurymachus, who warmed the bow by the fire to make it more supple. But he failed to string it and threw it to the floor in anger.

Now Antinous suggested an interval for more wine-drinking. But the crafty Odysseus shuffled forward. "Give me the bow, good sirs," he cried. "Let me see if there is any strength left in these old arms of mine." He raised his wrinkled beggar arms on high.

The suitors laughed and shouted. But, at a sign from Telemachus, Eumaeus walked forward, took the bow from the floor and put it in the hands of his master Odysseus.

Spearman
Odysseus's spear would have resembled the one shown above. A spear was a main weapon of a hoplite, a Greek warrior.

With arrow after arrow, Odysseus picked off the suitors one by one.

Odysseus took his stand. He twisted the bow in his hands, testing it. Then, as easily as a musician strings a lyre, he bent the great bow and strung it. His right hand twanged the bowstring and it sang like a swallow.

In the silence that followed he picked an arrow, set it to the string, drew it back and let fly. It sped perfectly down the line of the twelve axes. Odysseus turned to his son Telemachus and said: "The contest is over. The feasting is done. Now is the time for dancing."

Odysseus nodded. That was the signal.

Athene raised her right hand and the beggar was revealed to everybody in the hall as the mighty Odysseus.

"The contest is over and won!" he shouted. "Now let's try another target." He aimed an arrow at Antinous, who was sipping from a golden cup of wine. The shaft hissed through the air and transfixed the man's throat.

The suitors rose and looked around them, but all their weapons had been hidden by Telemachus. They heard a voice like thunder: "I am Odysseus. Yesterday you ate my food and drank my wine and insulted my wife. But today – you die."

Big Eurymachus tried to rally the suitors and was rewarded with an arrow in the chest. Next Amphinomus attacked Odysseus with his sword, but Telemachus dropped him with a spear between the shoulder blades.

With arrow after speeding arrow, Odysseus picked off the suitors one by one. And when his arrows ran out he picked up two huge spears and set to work with those.

Meanwhile the swineherd and cowherd were slicing away with their swords on either side of the brave Telemachus. All down the hall lay piles of dying suitors.

Six suitors found their spears and took aim at Odysseus. But, perching on a rafter in the shape of an owl, Athene raised her left wing. The six spears clattered harmlessly to the floor.

The killing continued until Athene suddenly appeared as herself, walking majestically through the air. When they saw the great goddess, the few suitors still left alive stampeded out of that hall like a herd of cattle maddened by flies.

Helmet
This both protected the head and struck fear into an enemy.

Breastplate
A soldier's breastplate was made of bronze, and might be molded to suit the wearer's physique. Its front and back sections were joined by leather straps.

Chapter fifteen

Husband and wife

Arcadia
Legend says that Arcadia on the Greek mainland (the central Peloponnese) is where Odysseus made his sacrifice to Poseidon.

THE OLD NURSE RAN UPSTAIRS to tell her mistress the amazing news, "Wake up, Penelope, my baby," she cried. "Your husband Odysseus has come home. And he's killed those villains who've been eating you out of house and home."

"It's true," she shouted as Penelope protested. "That beggar in the hall – it was him in disguise!"

Penelope was dazed. She walked down to the hall – now cleared of bodies. Odysseus sat by the fire, staring into the flames. Penelope sat down opposite him. There was a long silence.

"So many years," Penelope thought to herself. "I don't know what to say. I don't know what to do. But if this man really is Odysseus, I'll soon find out."

Finally Odysseus spoke. "What a woman! No other wife could have resisted touching her husband after nineteen years apart. If you don't care for me any more, tell my old nurse to find a bed where I can sleep alone."

"All right," said Penelope, planning to test him. "Eurycleia! Fetch the bed that Odysseus made. Bring it out here by the fire!"

Odysseus shouted: "How in the name of Hades can she fetch that bed? I carved it out of a living tree – it's the only bed in the world with roots and branches!"

He knew the secret. Now Penelope was sure of him. Her heart melted. She flung her arms around his neck and kissed him again and again. He wept and held her close in his arms. Then they walked slowly to the great bed made out of a tree. And they were as happy as they ever had been.

But next morning Odysseus had to go on his pilgrimage to find a place where the people had never heard of the sea. He walked for many weeks, a long and heavy oar on his shoulder. At last he came to a village where a farmer called out to him: "Hey stranger, what's that funny spade you're carrying?"

Odysseus stopped and found that the villagers had never heard of the sea. So he planted his oar in the ground. From the farmer he bought a fine ram, a bull, and a boar. He sacrificed all three to the sea god Poseidon, asking forgiveness for the blinding of Polyphemus. Poseidon, at last, was satisfied. Odysseus bought a strong horse and rode home.

Odysseus returned to a most happy reunion with his old father Laertes, who had been kept in hiding for years by Eumaeus after threats from the suitors. Laertes was overjoyed to see his long-lost son and behaved more like an eight-year-old than a man of eighty. All was well until Telemachus saw, approaching the house of Odysseus, a small army of heavily armed men. They were the relations of the slaughtered suitors, on a mission of vengeance.

They chanted their hatred of Odysseus. Telemachus summoned all the servants. Even old Laertes fetched a sword and waved it threateningly at the advancing forces.

It seemed as if the result of the first massacre would be a second massacre. And then perhaps a third, in revenge for the second? And so on. In the home of the gods, Mount Olympus, Athene pleaded with the great god Zeus: "Are these horrors to go on forever?"

Mentor
In Homer's original version, Odysseus asked his friend Mentor, who had a reputation for great wisdom, to act as a tutor to his baby son, Telemachus. Mentor died while Odysseus was away from home. The character is still remembered today: a "mentor" means a trusted advisor.

Zeus smiled. "Athene, if you can make a peace treaty between these families, so be it."

So, just as the warriors were about to clash swords in a terrible collision of metal and flesh, the goddess Athene appeared between them like a statue carved out of the living sunlight. She cried out to them with a great cry, "No! Drop your weapons! You have done enough killing!" Both sides dropped their swords and spears to the ground in fear and wonder at that great voice. Athene assumed the form of Mentor, the wisest of men. All the warriors on both sides gathered around and listened carefully as Mentor reasoned gently with them and established peace between the two parties.

Penelope ran forward, took the hand of Odysseus and smiled
him. "At last," she said. "Now you can stop being a hero and be
farmer and live with your family."

Odysseus kissed her and laughed. That evening Penelope and
dysseus sat outside their house enjoying a dish of olives and a
ink of wine. They could see Telemachus plowing and the seagulls
llowing his plow. Slowly the scarlet sun sank into
e ocean and Odysseus said: "I think I'm going to enjoy peace."

*Athene appeared
between them like a
statue carved out of
living sunlight.*

Fruit of peace
*The olive tree had symbolic
meaning for the ancient
Greeks. An olive branch
was a token of peace, and a
crown of olive leaves was a
token of victory. This 2500-
year-old pot shows workers
harvesting olives.*

ODYSSEUS'S JOURNEY

EVER SINCE ANCIENT TIMES, the many thrilling episodes in *The Odyssey* have inspired artists of all kinds. However, the story has also captured ordinary people's imaginations – to the extent that places all over the Mediterranean region have become identified with certain events. Attempts have also been made to trace Odysseus's route. This map shows a possible course he could have taken on his journey home, taking in various places associated with the legend.

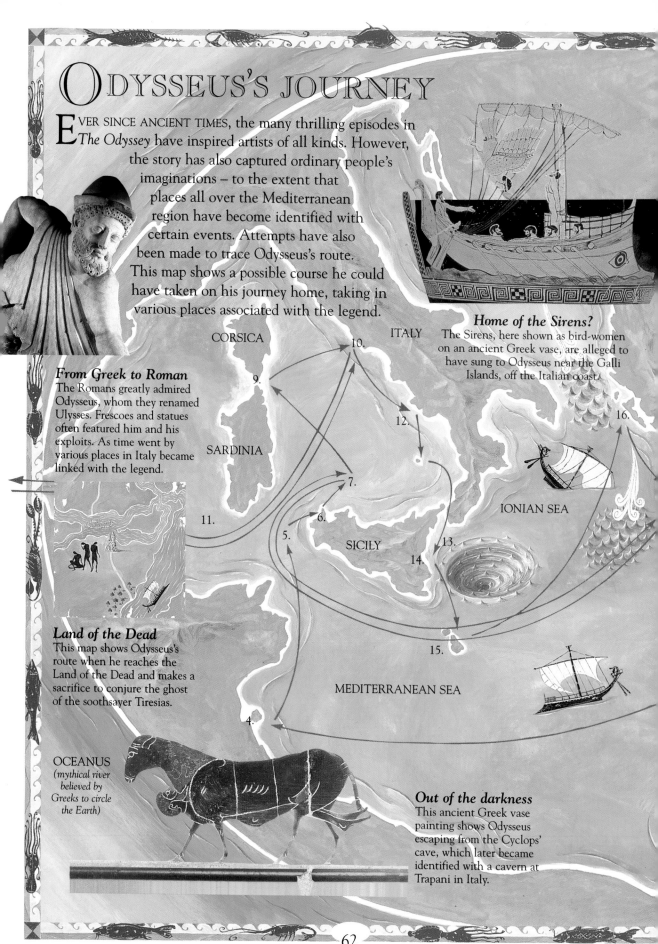

Home of the Sirens?
The Sirens, here shown as bird-women on an ancient Greek vase, are alleged to have sung to Odysseus near the Galli Islands, off the Italian coast.

From Greek to Roman
The Romans greatly admired Odysseus, whom they renamed Ulysses. Frescoes and statues often featured him and his exploits. As time went by various places in Italy became linked with the legend.

Land of the Dead
This map shows Odysseus's route when he reaches the Land of the Dead and makes a sacrifice to conjure the ghost of the soothsayer Tiresias.

OCEANUS
(mythical river believed by Greeks to circle the Earth)

Out of the darkness
This ancient Greek vase painting shows Odysseus escaping from the Cyclops' cave, which later became identified with a cavern at Trapani in Italy.

CORSICA

ITALY

SARDINIA

SICILY

IONIAN SEA

MEDITERRANEAN SEA

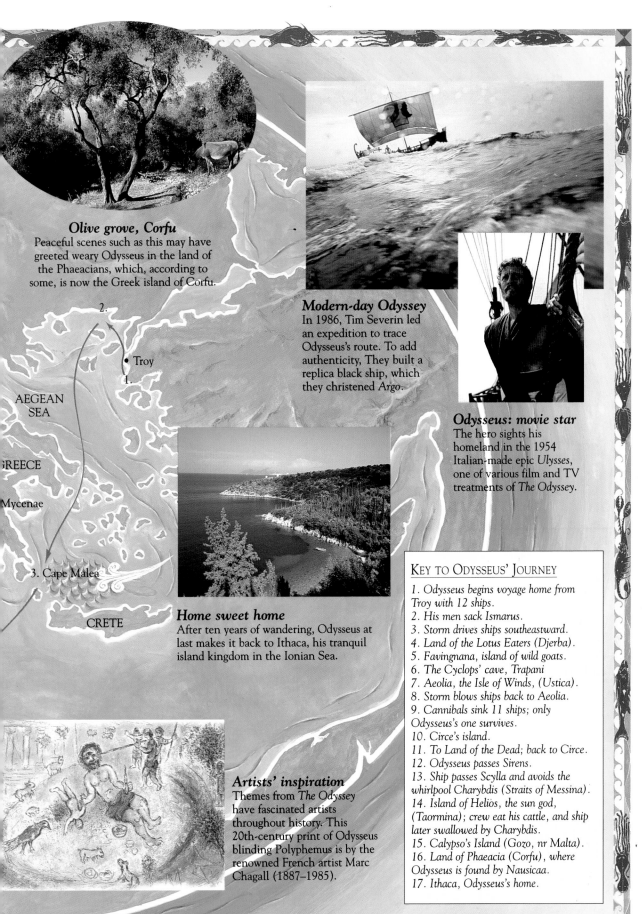

Olive grove, Corfu
Peaceful scenes such as this may have greeted weary Odysseus in the land of the Phaeacians, which, according to some, is now the Greek island of Corfu.

2.

• Troy

1.

AEGEAN SEA

GREECE

Mycenae

3. Cape Malea

CRETE

Modern-day Odyssey
In 1986, Tim Severin led an expedition to trace Odysseus's route. To add authenticity, They built a replica black ship, which they christened *Argo*.

Odysseus: movie star
The hero sights his homeland in the 1954 Italian-made epic *Ulysses*, one of various film and TV treatments of *The Odyssey*.

Home sweet home
After ten years of wandering, Odysseus at last makes it back to Ithaca, his tranquil island kingdom in the Ionian Sea.

Artists' inspiration
Themes from *The Odyssey* have fascinated artists throughout history. This 20th-century print of Odysseus blinding Polyphemus is by the renowned French artist Marc Chagall (1887–1985).

KEY TO ODYSSEUS' JOURNEY

1. Odysseus begins voyage home from Troy with 12 ships.
2. His men sack Ismarus.
3. Storm drives ships southeastward.
4. Land of the Lotus Eaters (Djerba).
5. Favignana, island of wild goats.
6. The Cyclops' cave, Trapani
7. Aeolia, the Isle of Winds, (Ustica).
8. Storm blows ships back to Aeolia.
9. Cannibals sink 11 ships; only Odysseus's one survives.
10. Circe's island.
11. To Land of the Dead; back to Circe.
12. Odysseus passes Sirens.
13. Ship passes Scylla and avoids the whirlpool Charybdis (Straits of Messina).
14. Island of Helios, the sun god, (Taormina); crew eat his cattle, and ship later swallowed by Charybdis.
15. Calypso's Island (Gozo, nr Malta).
16. Land of Phaeacia (Corfu), where Odysseus is found by Nausicaa.
17. Ithaca, Odysseus's home.

Acknowledgments

Picture Credits

The publishers would like to thank the following for their kind permission to reproduce the photographs.
t=top, b=bottom, l=left, r=right, a=above

AKG London: 9tl,10tl, 62tl
Bridgeman Art Library: 8cl, crb, 10bl, 12tl,14cl,20tl, 21cr, 24tl, 29tr, 52bl, 54tl, 61br, 62tr
Fitzwilliam Museum, University of Cambridge: 50cl
Phillips Auctioneers, London: 63bl
York City Art Gallery: 33tr
Bruce Coleman Collection: 51cr
Sylvia Cordaiy: 19tl
DK Picture Library/British Museum: 26bl, 31tl, tr, 57tr, cr, 62bl
ET Archive: 8cr, 9c,16cl, 31bl, 48tl
Mary Evans Picture Library: 36tl, 41br, 54bl
Ronald Grant Archive: 12cl, 30tr
Sonia Halliday: 9br, 19tr, 31cr, 58tl
Robert Harding Picture Library: 42tl

Kobal Collection: 9cl, bl, 63cra
Scala: 8tl, b, 9tr, 30cl, br,46tl
Tim Severin: 6-7, 63tr
Spectrum Colour Library: 32tl
Tony Stone Images: 30tc
Travel Ink: 63c

Jacket:
Scala: Front tr
Bridgeman Art Library: Front tl
DK Picture Library/British Museum: Back bl
David Sillitoe: Back flap tl

Additional photography by: Dave King, Nick Nicholls, Kim Sayer

Dorling Kindersley would particularly like to thank the following people:
Tanya Tween and Joanna Pocock for design assitance; Gary Hyde and Laia Roses for jacket design; Jill Bunyan for DTP design; Linda Dare for Production assistance; Sally Hamilton in DK Picture Library.